MERRY LOVER

Crime and Passion, Novella

Mary Lancaster

ARE YOU SIGNED UP FOR DRAGONBLADE'S BLOG?

You'll get the latest news and information on exclusive giveaways, exclusive excerpts, coming releases, sales, free books, cover reveals and more.

Check out our complete list of authors, too!

No spam, no junk. That's a promise!

Sign Up Here

www.dragonbladepublishing.com

Dearest Reader;

Thank you for your support of a small press. At Dragonblade Publishing, we strive to bring you the highest quality Historical Romance from some of the best authors in the business. Without your support, there is no 'us', so we sincerely hope you adore these stories and find some new favorite authors along the way.

Happy Reading!

CEO, Dragonblade Publishing

Vienna Waltz
Vienna Woods
Vienna Dawn

Blackhaven Brides Series
The Wicked Baron
The Wicked Lady
The Wicked Rebel
The Wicked Husband
The Wicked Marquis
The Wicked Governess
The Wicked Spy
The Wicked Gypsy
The Wicked Wife
Wicked Christmas (A Novella)
The Wicked Waif
The Wicked Heir
The Wicked Captain
The Wicked Sister

Unmarriageable Series
The Deserted Heart
The Sinister Heart
The Vulgar Heart
The Broken Heart
The Weary Heart
The Secret Heart
Christmas Heart

The Lyon's Den Connected World
Fed to the Lyon

De Wolfe Pack: The Series
The Wicked Wolfe
Vienna Wolfe

Also from Mary Lancaster
Madeleine

GOD REST YE MERRY, GENTLEMEN has always been one of my favourite Christmas carols. When I was a child, it seemed to personify the fun of Christmas, not least because of the idea of all these merry gentlemen (though a few ladies would have been good, too), resting from their jollity. But of course, the song is not really about merry gentlemen resting. It's all about where we put the comma!

Being one of the oldest carols in English, dating from at latest the sixteenth century, the language is a little arcane. "God rest you" here means not "sit down and have a kip" but "God keep you." In other words: God keep you happy, because the birth of Jesus saves us from straying toward the devil.

So, not *God rest you, merry gentlemen!* But *God rest you merry, gentlemen!* Although, as you will see, my heroine has some fun with that, too.

Incidentally, you can read more about Griz and Dragan in my Crime & Passion series, particularly in Book 1, *Mysterious Lover.*

ML

CHAPTER ONE

L ADY GRIZELDA TIZSA awoke in the warmth of delightful dreams. Still half-asleep, she rolled over in search of her husband—and found only a cold pillow and empty space.

Christmas Eve, and still, he was not home.

Missing Dragan was like an ache. She had never expected to spend their first Christmas as a married couple apart. Or with child, if she was honest, but both appeared to be her fate.

However, she refused to dwell on her difficulties. Since it was almost daylight, she reached for her spectacles and rose from her cozy bed into the freezing air of a winter's morning. Driven by cold and the slightly sick hunger of pregnancy, she sped through the motions of washing and dressing in her warmest old gown and several shawls before she bolted for the warmth of the kitchen to forage for breakfast.

Here, she was greeted with delight by Vicky, her affectionate yet haughty little greyhound whom she had named after the queen. Thanks to the stove, the kitchen was the warmest room in the house, so she fed the fire, set water to boil, and cut herself two thick slices of bread, which she slathered with butter and jam.

Before they had known Dragan would be trapped in Edinburgh by snowstorms, they had granted their maid and cook leave to spend Christmas with their own families, and both servants had left as planned yesterday. The idea of being completely alone together and looking after themselves had seemed fun at the time. But Dragan was a lot more practical than she, who had been brought up in a ducal household with maids and footmen so thick on the ground that she had purposely avoided them.

For the first time, she began to wish she had gone to the country with her family. She had to admit, it was lonely here, with just Vicky and the tiny creature growing within her.

But it was only Christmas Eve, and there was still time for Dragan to come home today. In the meantime, she sang to herself to keep her spirits up while she made tea and let Vicky into the pleasant, enclosed garden at the back of the house.

Theirs was an odd house for Mayfair. Neither as large nor as tall as its neighbors, it sprawled across a piece of land that had once belonged to the house behind them on Half Moon Street. There was something about freezing air at Christmas that set off a hundred pleasant memories. She inhaled deeply and kept singing.

God rest ye merry, gentlemen,
Let nothing you dismay.
For Jesus Christ our Savior was born on Christmas Day,
To save us all from Satan's power when we had gone astray.
Oh, tidings of comfort and joy,
Comfort and joy.
Oh, tidings of comfort and joy.

Vicky bolted back inside, and Griz closed the door and poured herself another cup of tea. She had a busy day ahead of her, but it was still early, and a bracing walk to the park with Vicky would be a good start.

And when I come home, Dragan might be here waiting for me. On that happy, if unlikely, hope, she donned her hat and warm wool cape, put Vicky on the leash, and unlocked the front door.

For once, the dog hung back as she opened it. Rather than darting enthusiastically through the smallest crack, she pulled back into the house. And Griz soon saw why.

A man sat on the ground against the wall, his silk hat beside him. But it was not Dragan. This man was older, his hair white with frost.

After her first start, she wondered why Vicky wasn't barking.

"Sir?" she asked in alarm. "Sir, can I help you?"

The man did not reply. Letting Vicky cower back into the house, she stepped outside and was relieved to see the man was smiling, a full, happy curve of the lips.

But the smile did not reach his eyes, which were open and staring.

Her belly stung, and she flung one comforting arm over it. "Oh, dear God," she whispered. She did not recognize the man. She had never seen him before in her life, but she was very afraid...

Crouching down, she forced herself to feel, as Dragan would, for the pulse in his neck. She could feel nothing but cold. There was frost on his hair, on his clothing. The man was dead, but from his smile had died very happy.

"God rest you, merry gentleman," she murmured irreverently, even while pity caught in her throat. "But what in the world are you doing at my front door? And what the *devil* am I supposed to do about you?"

The man was well to do. Beneath the frost, his clothes and his hat were of the finest quality, his overcoat, a fine, thick grey wool, with a fur collar. Something caught her eye, clinging to his coat, just behind the hand curled in his lap. It was small and white, and when she lifted it, it came easily. A single, white flower petal.

Without thought, she dropped it into her pocket and rose. Taking a deep breath, she pulled the front door closed and sped down the path, through the gate, and down the lane. She saw no one until she came on to Half Moon Street, where, toward Piccadilly, she saw Jake, the boy who swept the crossing and often ran messages for her and Dragan.

"Run and fetch a constable to my house," she begged him, thrusting a coin into his willing hand. "Tell him it's important that there is a dead man outside my house."

"Blimey." Awed, Jake propped his broom against the lamp post and bolted.

Griz hastened back to the house. She gave the dead man a wide berth, but even so, he drew her gaze. His smile was ridiculously happy, quite incongruous beneath the dead, lifeless eyes. She wondered if he had really died so merrily or if some odd, physical response to illness or pain had caused him to grimace. That seemed more likely.

She could see no blood, no obvious injury or tear to his clothing. But it seemed disrespectful to leave him on display. She opened the door with her key and closed it again behind her. Vicky was still cowering in the hallway. In need of comfort herself, Griz scooped her up and cuddled her.

"I know," she told her ruefully. "Not such a merry Christmas so far. Shall we find something to cover the face of the poor gentleman?"

Before she did that, she hastily cleaned out and set the fire in the drawing room, for she expected to be invaded by policemen and saw no reason for anyone else to freeze to death.

Was that really what had happened to her smiling gentleman? Had he sat there all night, freezing to death while she slept? She did not like that idea. It made her feel guilty as well as sad. But neither did it make much sense. He was not a friend or family member who had knocked on her door unheard. Nor was he some poor, homeless man without the means of shelter.

Or was he? Had he been robbed, attacked in the street, and bolted to this house for safety, only to die before he could raise an alarm?

She did not like that idea either.

She went upstairs and rummaged in the linen cupboard. For some reason, she chose a blanket, as if that would somehow make him warm.

He still sat upright, his head resting against the wall. She wondered if he would keel over with the weight of the blanket on his head. She began at his fine, polished shoes, and drew the blanket up over his legs to where one gloved hand lay in his lap, and paused, for a whole flower showed there now, its stem tucked between his fingers. A single Christmas rose.

That was not there before!

Abandoning the blanket, she ran down the garden path once more and glanced both ways up and down the lane. Was that a skirt disappearing into Half Moon Street?

She hesitated, curiosity, as always, her besetting sin, urging her to run after the vanishing skirt. But common sense told her the passer-by was as likely to have merely crossed the narrow lane as come from her front door.

Returning to the body, she hesitated again. It felt disrespectful to take the flower someone had clearly put there. Instead, she drew from her pocket the single petal she had found earlier and compared it to the flower in the dead man's hand.

The petal was the same shape, clearly from another Christmas rose. But her petal was pure white. The one in the corpse's fingers was tinged with pink. Frowning, she sat back on her heels. Then, with a quick glance over her shoulder to see if the awaited policeman approached, she felt inside the man's pockets.

She found a fat purse and a notecase, so it seemed he had not been robbed. She also found a card case, and although voices and footsteps now sounded in the lane, she whipped out one of the cards and shoved the case back in his pocket. Hastily, she covered him with the blanket—flower and all—draping the folds lightly over his head, which, to her relief, still did not move. Then she whisked herself inside the house again, took off her cloak and bonnet, and waited to be summoned.

CHAPTER TWO

ACCORDING TO HIS card, Mr. Sebastian Cartaret was the name of her dead gentleman, and the direction beneath was a city office, not a home address.

She barely had time to register that before a loud knock on the front door caused her to shove the card under the nearest book on her desk and march out to deal with whichever police constable Jake had dragged to the scene.

Two constables and a familiar man in a grey coat and bowler hat stood on her doorstep.

"Lady Grizelda," Inspector Harris said briskly. "Why am I not surprised?"

"Probably because Jake told you it was my house." She held the door wide. "Come in."

The inspector made a sign to his men to wait outside and walked into the house, taking off his hat.

"I did not expect someone of your rank quite so soon," she said, leading him into the drawing room.

"I happened to be with the constable when your lad came flying into us." The inspector's gaze flickered around the room, which probably looked eccentric to him, filled as it was with bookcases, and a large, business-like desk, as well as comfortable chairs and a sofa. Pencil drawings, including many of her, were scattered among the wall decorations. "Where is Mr. Tizsa?"

"Edinburgh," Griz replied, and was immediately deluged with fresh longing for his presence.

Inspector Harris blinked, finally surprised. "What is he doing there?"

"Attending lectures. He means to sit his medical examinations in the spring."

Harris held her gaze. "So, he went up there over Christmas?" Not by tone or even a flicker of a brow did he betray disbelief, and yet she knew it was there.

"He was meant to be home yesterday. They have snowstorms up in Scotland. You seem surprised, Inspector."

"I am. I had not imagined you the type of lady to be entertaining gentlemen in her husband's absence."

Griz flushed with more indignation than embarrassment. "I am not in the habit of entertaining dead gentlemen at any time! I found him there when I went out this morning."

"And who is he?"

Mr. Sebastian Cartaret. But to say so betrayed either that she knew him, which she didn't, or that she had taken evidence from the scene, which she undoubtedly had. But if he didn't know the man's name now, he soon would. There were plenty of cards. "I have no idea. I believe your resources are greater than mine."

"Then what was he doing at your house?"

"Sadly, I could not ask him."

One eyebrow rose. "You are very defensive, my lady."

She held his gaze. "Do you blame me? You seem to be implying some improper connection between the dead man and me."

"Is there one?"

"Of course, there is not! He clearly spent all last night *outside* the house, would you not agree?"

"Then you do not know him, have never seen him before?"

"Never."

"And you have no idea what he was doing here?"

"None. I suppose he could be a friend of Dragan's, but if so, I have never met him. He seems well to do, so if he had no home nearby, he would have had no difficulty staying at a hotel. Or his club, if he had one. Do you know how he died? I saw no sign of injury."

"There seems to be none. At least nothing obvious. It's possible his heart simply gave out, or there is some hidden damage still to be found."

Like poison? A poisoned flask of brandy taken away by his killer? Possible, although there was no evidence of such, and either way, why at her house?

"We'll know more after the post-mortem examination," Inspector Harris stated.

"Perhaps he was taken ill in the street," Griz speculated, "and came here for help, then collapsed before he could even knock on the door."

"Perhaps," the inspector said doubtfully. "Only why would he come up this lane, which leads only to your house? Why not knock on the nearest door in Half Moon Street?"

"It does not make sense," she agreed.

"Unless he was coming here specifically."

"I did not invite him," she said firmly.

"Hmm. Forgive me, but he seems a bit well to do for one of Tizsa's friends."

Griz sighed. "That's what I thought," she agreed. "But one never knows about Dragan's friends. One of the Hungarian refugees might know him. Or Dr. Cordell." Even saying the words seemed to reinforce that he was completely alien in her life or Dragan's.

And yet, someone had placed a rose in his dead hands only minutes after she had left him. Someone who had been watching her? She shivered. Someone who had killed him in a manner yet undiscovered? Someone, certainly, who knew him. The gesture seemed far too personal for mere pity or respect. And, of course, there was the other petal to be considered, too.

"I beg your pardon?" she said vaguely, realizing Inspector Harris had been talking through her reverie.

"I asked you where you were last night," he said patiently.

"I was here, of course."

"All night?"

How strange to be considered a suspect, at last. The first time they had met, she should have been the chief suspect in the murder of her maid, and yet they had arrested Dragan. "Yes," she replied firmly. "From five o'clock yesterday afternoon."

"And what about your maid? Or any other servants? Perhaps you would just ring for them?"

"There's no one else here," Griz admitted. "Our maid and cook have both gone to their families for Christmas."

He could not quite prevent the widening of his eyes. "You are here *alone*?"

"Completely," she said defiantly.

She realized how odd it looked. She, a duke's daughter, alone in her house after sending her servants away, and a man who was not her husband sitting familiarly by her front door. Dead.

For the first time, she wondered if even Dragan would believe she did not know the dead man. That really was a horrific contemplation that even the baby seemed to object to, for her stomach tightened. Surely even the tiniest seed of doubt could affect the happiness of their marriage, especially now, for they had *always* trusted each other before. At least, after the initial skirmish over the body they had discovered together last spring...

Well, it clearly behooved her to find out who the dead man was and what, if any, reason he had for being where he was. Quickly. Preferably before Dragan came home.

"When will the post-mortem be carried out?" she asked.

"Probably after Christmas now. Unless the doctor has time today, which is unlikely."

"Will you let me know what he says? I would be obliged. Even a note would do. I wish Dragan were here."

Perhaps he heard the genuine need in her voice, for his eyes actually softened for the first time since she had opened the door.

"So do I. You should not be alone, my lady. Can you not go to your family?"

"They are all in the country." She smiled, lest he begin to pity her. "But I have friends I can call on. If you learn anything, I will still be here to receive your message."

He nodded and turned to go. But he had one more question to fling at her.

"Did you and Tizsa quarrel before he went to Scotland?"

"No," she said ruefully. "But I wish I had gone with him."

⋙✦⋘

WHY HAD SHE not? Why had she allowed a month apart when it was one of only a few left to them before the baby's birth in the spring? The knowledge that he would be focused on studies in which she could not share? The desire to prove that she was not afraid to be alone and pregnant? A need to show him that the baby did not make her more dependent on him?

All of those things, perhaps. And he had not tried to persuade her, merely asked and accepted her refusal. But she had told Harris the truth. There had been no quarrel, just a tender if tearful parting, a promise to write, and then passionately looking forward to his return for Christmas and their "secret" time alone together.

And now, she longed for him with a force that made her whole body tingle, from her insides to her fingertips.

In the end, she ran out of time to take Vicky for a walk, for she spent too long thinking and staring at Mr. Cartaret's card and the rose petal. And she may have thought of Dragan, though wishing would not bring him to her any quicker. She wondered if there were even trains running still from Scotland.

While she thought and speculated and missed her husband's company, as well as his sharp, creative mind, she did her best to decorate the house for Christmas, hanging trails of ivy above the mantelpieces in the drawing room and the dining room and adding as much bright holly as she could find. She hauled a large, fallen tree branch from the back garden through the kitchen and into the hall. Here, she abandoned it temporarily under the step ladder, for she suddenly realized the time and had to run upstairs and change into a more festive gown.

She had promised to attend the Christmas party in St. Giles for the children of the poor and denizens of the soup kitchen where she helped the local, charitably minded vicar, Mr. Wells.

So she donned her dark green dress with its many wide petticoats and wore it with the bright red Paisley shawl, which had been a gift from her sister Azalea. Then, she shoved her violin into its case and said farewell to the sulking Vicky.

It was on her mind, as she hurried down the lane, to look out for the flower sellers, who were largely selling holly and mistletoe, along with a few expensive hothouse flowers for those who could afford it. But some might sell Christmas roses, like the one in the dead man's hand.

Suddenly, she stopped in the lane and turned back. From here, she could see part of the garden belonging to the house on the other side of her back garden. Belonging to the people who had once lived in her house. Westley was their name. When they had inherited the bigger house from Westley's parents, they had sold off the smaller dwelling.

And in their side garden, visible over the lane wall, was a Christmas rose bush laden with blooms of just the right shade of pink.

CHAPTER THREE

F ROM THE BREAKFAST parlor of her home in Half Moon Street, Mrs. Elizabeth Westley could see out the window across her back garden to that of the smaller house in the lane. There was no real need for her to do so. It wasn't as if she could see Sebastian sitting and smiling at the front of the house. For one thing, she had seen policemen come up and down the lane. The last time, they had left bearing a covered stretcher.

Her chest constricted with grief and guilt and a thousand emotions she had no name for. If the servants or, worse, her husband, found her staring so fixedly out of the window, they would think she was ill. And yet, she could not bring herself to move away. Some movement at the corner of her eye drew her gaze to the right, to the patch of lane that was visible from the window. Someone was walking briskly toward Half Moon Street, and yes, it was Mrs. Tizsa. Or Lady Grizelda, the duke's daughter who now lived with her Hungarian husband in Elizabeth's old home.

Elizabeth had been glad it was they who had bought the house when William, her husband, had sold it. They had seemed an eccentric couple but loving, and, of course, it did one's consequence no harm to have a duke's family buy one's cast-offs.

Sebastian had been the one difficulty.

A knock on the breakfast room door made her jump as she turned to face the intruder. James, the footman, entered, bearing a silver tray with a calling card.

Elizabeth stared at it. It said simply *Grizelda Tizsa,* without title, just her address, *Half Moon Street Lane.*

"The lady is waiting, ma'am," James prompted. "I told her I wasn't sure you were at home."

It was tempting, very tempting to deny herself and carry on hiding. But one did not deny oneself to a duke's daughter without very good reason, and it was imperative she behave as expected.

"You had better bring her ladyship to the drawing room," Elizabeth said quickly.

She waited, trying to quell the fast beating of her heart until she heard James's footsteps and the lighter tread of a lady with the accompanying swishing of skirts. By then, she had herself better in hand and even pinned a pleasant, gratified smiled on her face as she left the breakfast parlor and walked along the passage and into the drawing room.

"Lady Grizelda," she greeted her with courtesy. "What a pleasant surprise! So sorry to keep you waiting. Merry Christmas to you!"

"And to you," Lady Grizelda said with a quick smile as she returned the curtsey. She wore a warm, flowing cape over a gown that looked to be of good velvet, from what she could see beneath the cape, though it lacked the flounces and frills necessary to make it truly fashionable. In fact, considering her rank, she made very few concessions to fashion. She even wore spectacles, which seemed to gleam malevolently at Elizabeth.

"Forgive my calling so early and uninvited," Lady Grizelda said brightly, "but a very strange thing happened this morning, and it suddenly struck me that you might be able to help."

"Of course, if I can." Elizabeth hoped the smile on her face wasn't looking too strained. It was very hard to read Lady Grizelda's expression, perhaps because her spectacles veiled her eyes too much. Elizabeth, having met her only once before, had never decided whether or not she was pretty. She was young and lively, of course, and had a certain though vague appeal, but if His Grace, her father, had thrown her away on a penniless Hungarian refugee, it said little for her charm or intelligence. "Won't you sit down?"

"Thank you. Believe it or not," her ladyship said almost apologetically, taking the nearest chair, "I opened my front door this morning to find a dead man propped up against the wall."

"Oh, my dear!" Elizabeth exclaimed. "How awful for you! Do you know who he was?"

"That was what I was hoping you could tell me," Lady Grizelda confided. "You see, he is quite unknown to my household, and it struck me that he might be known to yours. I wondered if he had not realized you now lived here."

"Oh, I shouldn't think so. Both my husband I told everyone about our move."

"He was quite a tall gentleman, in his late forties, I would say, handsome, with a fine head of greying hair. He was very well dressed, clearly a gentleman of means."

"He does not sound like anyone I know."

"Ah, well, it was a faint hope," her ladyship said, rising to her feet.

Relieved, Elizabeth roused herself. "Perhaps you would care for a cup of tea?"

"Oh, no, thank you. I am expected elsewhere and must not linger. But I thank you for your kindness."

"His...body is not still at your door, is it?" Elizabeth asked, knowing perfectly well it was not.

"Oh, no, the police took him away. I hope I have not spoiled your day."

"Of course not. It is you who must have been upset by such a gruesome discovery."

"I was, actually," her ladyship admitted. She smiled again. "But it is Christmas, and I am determined to enjoy the festivities." She walked to the door and paused, her fingers on the handle, and glanced back over her shoulder. "I don't suppose you know the name Cartaret, do you?"

It felt like a knife in the heart. Panic surged. *She knows! She knows!* But years of dissembling had been good practice, and somehow, she kept the smile pinned to her face. "No, I don't believe so. Why?"

"I am so forgetful," Lady Grizelda said vaguely and entirely unhelpfully. "Goodbye, Mrs. Westley. Merry Christmas."

As soon as the door closed behind her, Elizabeth sank into her chair and buried her head in her hands. *I am found out. Somehow, she knows.*

FROM OLD HABITS—OR were they new?—Grizelda had deliberately withheld the name of the dead man when she had described him to Mrs. Westley. Most people, surely, if asked whether or not they knew someone, would have asked for his name. She hadn't.

And from Grizelda's physical description, which could have fit any number of gentlemen in London, Mrs. Westley had declared him unknown to her.

Both of those things she found suspicious. But the lady, whom she barely knew, may just have been uninterested or wished to avoid anything to do with such an unsavory incident as discovering a dead man at one's front door. And Griz had seen in her neighbor no sign of recognition at the name, only a strained and well-hidden desire to be rid of Griz. The woman was hiding *something*, she was sure, but not necessarily an act of murder or even a knowledge of the dead man.

On her way to the hackney stand, Griz spoke to a flower girl who was, indeed, selling Christmas roses, both white and pink.

"Will you save me a bunch of each?" Griz asked her, handing over some coins. "I'll collect them on my way home this afternoon. I suppose you must have sold lots of these today."

"A few, ma'am."

"I don't suppose you recall selling any last night or early this morn-ing? Perhaps to a tall, well-dressed gentleman with greying hair and a fur collar on his coat?"

"No, ma'am," the girl replied apologetically. "I were sold out be-fore dark yesterday. Sold a few this morning, though."

"To anyone in particular?" Griz asked. "To any ladies? Anyone who walked off toward Half Moon Street?"

"Not sure, ma'am," the girl said uneasily. "I don't think so."

"Never mind. Thank you, I'll be back later for the flowers."

FOR A TIME, Griz forgot about Sebastian Cartaret and her own loneliness, and if the ache of missing Dragan didn't vanish, at least it settled into the background, as she helped make a couple of special hours for some of the poorest people in London.

While the adults who came along were given tea and sandwiches, the children played games. Then Griz got out her violin, and everyone danced to her music. The pure happiness on the faces of people who had nothing, even hope in most cases, whose lives were destined to be unutterably hard, brought tears to her eyes. She had to fight not to shed them. She smiled instead, glad to have helped create this moment.

In high spirits, the children were then seated at the prepared tables and wolfed down their festive luncheon. The adults helped themselves from the buffet. And in the relative silence of some serious eating, Griz gazed speculatively up at the vicar.

He was a good man, whose fame for charitable works was spread-ing. He received donations from all over the city nowadays, from the exceedingly wealthy to those who could merely spare a few coins for those less fortunate. In the absence of her family, who, between them, probably knew all the wealthy people in the country, the vicar might well be her best hope.

"I don't suppose," she said, "that you have ever come across a gentleman called Sebastian Cartaret?"

"Cartaret," he repeated. "Oh yes. Old family with land in Leicestershire. But Sebastian is quite the interesting character."

"He owns the land?"

"Oh, no, he's one of the younger sons, but he turned out to have a head for business. Made a vast fortune from investing in everything from banks to cotton mills and shipping. And now he seems to be giving it all away again. It was he who donated the bulk of the money for the school. And as a result, we were able to make the Christmas party a little more lavish than normal."

"Then he is a good man? Not the sort to inspire ill-feeling?"

The vicar blinked. "I don't suppose you make that amount of money without creating some ill-feeling. Jealousy, for one! But yes, I would say he is a good man."

"You know him personally?"

"I met him several times. Rather liked him, actually. Happy, cheerful person. And not, like some, full of pride in his own charity. He just seemed to want to give others a chance. Why, what is your interest in him?"

Griz swallowed. "I found him dead on my doorstep this morning."

"Oh, my dear Lady Griz," he said in quick concern.

"No, no, I'm fine, though I confess it was something of a shock. But I have no idea why he was there."

"And, of course, that bothers you. What does Dragan think?"

"Dragan isn't home yet," she said as brightly as she could manage. "So, I am focusing on the problem of my dead man to keep me busy. Was he married? Did he have children?"

"No. He never married. But he gave every indication of enjoying his life."

"Wine, women, and song?"

"I would say so."

She smiled a little tremulously. "Then he really was a merry gentleman."

This seemed to baffle the vicar, but Griz was suddenly distracted by a small child across the table who had crammed so much food in her mouth that she seemed likely to choke. She charged to the rescue.

When the food was all gone, everyone gathered around the decorated tree. Griz and other helpers lit the candles while the vicar told the story of Jesus's birth. As the gifts beneath the tree were distributed to the awed children, it struck Griz that Sebastian Cartaret had largely paid for them.

Oh yes, she owed him at least the courtesy of finding out the truth about his death.

CHAPTER FOUR

O N HER WAY home, Griz stopped off in Covent Garden, where she had asked a few of the flower sellers about people buying Christmas roses from them yesterday. She described Sebastian Cartaret, even called him by name.

None knew the name, though one girl said, "I did sell Christmas roses to a man like that. Very smart nob, he were."

"What color were they?" Griz asked, but the girl didn't know and couldn't tell her any more about the man, whom she couldn't recall seeing before. In fact, the description fitted so many men that Griz was not even confident this had been Cartaret. Still, she bought some Christmas roses from the girl by way of gratitude.

"You want to be careful with them, my lady," a familiar voice said in her ear. "Don't let your little dog chew them—they're poison."

"Nell!" She turned to greet the young woman with pleasure. "You're looking well."

Nell wrinkled her nose. "Looking respectable, you mean."

It was true that while her clothing was still brightly colored, it now covered her person.

"That, too," Griz agreed. "Are you still helping out with the children round the corner? George and Jilly?"

"Cooking their Christmas dinner tomorrow and having it with them. And their father. He wants to marry me."

"Do you want to marry him?"

Nell tossed her head. "Might as well if I can't have your man."

Griz laughed and thrust one bunch of the Christmas roses at her. "Merry Christmas, Nell! Compliments of the season to your new family!"

She left Covent Garden delighted for Nell, but at the same time, her words—*they're poison*—had her itching to be home among her books.

Inevitably, as she marched up the lane, at last, flowers in one hand, violin in the other, her heartbeat quickened at the possibility of finding Dragan had returned in her absence. She could not resist glancing up at the Westleys' house as she passed. Did she imagine the face darting back from the window?

Just as she had left the church hall, she had asked the vicar if he knew the Westleys, too. "He is a banker, I believe," she told him, "and thrives well enough to have a house in Half Moon Street."

But the Westleys were not, the vicar said, among his charity's donors, so there was no connection there.

Griz hurried up the garden path and let herself into the house with her key.

"Dragan?" she called, but there was no sign of his coat and hat in the hall, no bags dumped at the foot of the stairs. She knew he was not there. There was no *sense* of him in the air that felt suddenly stale and cold without him.

Comforted by Vicky's enthusiastic welcome, she made a fuss of the dog before she went and found vases for her flowers and distributed them between the drawing room and the dining room. Then, she returned to the drawing room with a cup of teaand began to scour the bookshelves for botanical works.

Nell was right. The roots, stems, and leaves of the *helleborus niger*—commonly known as the Christmas rose—were indeed poisonous. If eaten, they could be fatal for animals and could make a human very ill.

Griz sat back, frowning. She wasn't sure this took her any further forward. She couldn't imagine Cartaret eating leaves, which, in conjunction with some other illness, might just have made him ill enough to die. Nor could she imagine the respectable Mrs. Westley, for all the secrets she might possess, cramming them into his mouth and making him swallow them.

For one thing, such behavior would hardly make him smile.

If the smile were a smile.

Nor could she think of a motive. She knew of no connection between them, except that Mrs. Westley possessed a Christmas rose bush.

Why would anyone have placed a rose in his hand after his death? Respect? Pity? Love? Guilt?

And what of the single white petal? What was the significance of that?

She imagined it spilling out of his mouth as he ate the rest of the plant and jumped to her feet, shaking her head with almost angry impatience.

The short winter day was drawing to a close. She needed to light the candles for another long evening without Dragan.

Or...she could go out and look for more Christmas roses. Mrs. Westley's would not be the only one in Mayfair. Decisively, she resumed her cape and bonnet, put Vicky on the leash, and went for a long walk.

⇒⟩⟩⟩⟨⟨⟨⇐

"HOW BEAUTIFUL YOU have made the house!" Elizabeth Westley's husband beamed at her with genuine delight as he bent and kissed her cheek. His neat mustache tickled her skin.

"I wanted to have it done before you came home," she replied. "A glass of sherry before dinner?"

"Delightful. It is Christmas, after all."

William Westley was not an immoderate man. He drank rarely and never to excess. He was a good and considerate husband and an excellent father to their grown-up daughters, both of whom had now made good marriages and lived in the country. Elizabeth lacked for nothing in terms of either affection or material goods. And yet, she had long suffered from the feeling of being left behind.

William's career had never quite reached the stellar heights her father had predicted. Elizabeth's friends all had homes at least as grand as hers. In fact, for years, she and William had lived in the funny little house where Lady Grizelda and her foreign husband now resided. They had only moved into this one when they had inherited it from William's parents.

And now her daughters had gone, leaving her behind again.

She blamed Sebastian Cartaret for her constant discontent. Perhaps, now that he was dead, she would finally find peace.

And William… She brought him his glass of sherry and sat down opposite him. She could not bear William to know about Sebastian. He was so good, so trusting. And she so…evil.

"Have you heard the awful rumor, by the by?" William asked when he had tasted his sherry with appreciation.

"What rumor, my dear?"

"That a man's body was found at the front of our old house. Poor Lady Grizelda discovered it, and her husband is not even home to comfort her. It must have been awful for her."

"Awful," Elizabeth repeated. "I didn't realize she was alone there."

"No, well, I hope she has gone to her family for Christmas," William said, "for it can't be comfortable to know a man has been murdered at your front door!"

"Murdered?" she repeated hoarsely.

"According to rumor," he said apologetically. "I didn't mean to worry you with it because it's probably not even true. But I shall be checking personally that all the doors and windows are locked tonight.

Even if it is Christmas, the wicked will remain wicked."

Elizabeth cringed in fear for her immortal soul.

GRIZ SPENT A long time wandering the gas-lit streets and the gardens that graced the large squares from Russell to Grosvenor. She found several Christmas rose bushes, even a few of similar shade to the one left with the body.

The trouble was, Griz didn't really know what she was looking for. She spoke to a few people also walking their dogs in the squares, remarking on the beauty of the roses. She even joined some carol singers in order to peer into people's houses and observe the owners and servants who came to listen. But she was floundering in the dark, without any real idea what she was looking for.

In fact, she told herself severely, *you are wasting your time because you don't want to go home to the empty house and face a miserable Christmas alone.*

She worried for Dragan. Somewhere, she suspected Sebastian Cartaret was a mere distraction for her, and he deserved more from her. Not just because she hadn't heard him dying outside her house, but because he was a good man and deserved justice though it would not bring him back.

It had grown bitterly cold by the time she trudged back up Half Moon Street. Even Vicky had slowed up, plodding beside Griz and not even troubling to lunge at the odd passing cat.

Warm light glowed from the front of the Westleys' house. The lane to her own house was dark, the house unwelcoming. But at least the frosty night provided some starlight, enough to find the front door.

She stopped dead, her heart lurching, for the dark outline of a man could be seen, sitting against the wall, exactly where the body of Sebastian Cartaret had been. Her hand flew to her stomach, a hundred nameless fears flooding her. She did not believe in ghosts, and yet there he sat, still as death, as though admonishing her. Not only had she let him die, she hadn't even found out what had happened.

She crept forward, never taking her eyes from him, praying he was a figment of her tired imagination, which would dissolve into the night as she approached.

It didn't.

But at least the ghost sat in a different position than the corpse. Though his back was also against the wall, his knees were drawn up to let his head rest on them. He didn't seem to move or even breathe.

And then, suddenly, his head jerked up, and he looked right at her.

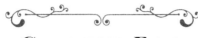

CHAPTER FIVE

A SOB RIPPED from Grizelda's throat. Without conscious thought, she flung herself across the distance between them, landing on top of him and his arms closed around her, her one true haven. But his skin was icy under her lips, shocking her back to reality.

"Dragan! How long have you been here? Why are you sitting here in the cold?" Hauling herself out of his lap, she stumbled to her feet, grasping his hand to pull him up.

"I left my key behind," he said, catching the delirious Vicky with one hand while he took Grizelda's hand with the other and rose. He had been sitting on one of his bags. "I think I fell asleep."

"I thought you were a ghost," she said shakily, pushing her key into the lock with trembling fingers.

"Why would I be a ghost?" He sounded faintly amused, though also, being Dragan, curious.

"I'll tell you later." She was reluctant to release his hand, but he extricated it long enough to pull off his gloves and light the lamp in the hall. While Griz lit the candle beside it, he retrieved his bags and his hat and closed the front door with his hip.

That done, he deposited his bags at the foot of the steps and looked about him, smiling. "How festive."

"I nearly didn't bother," she admitted. "I thought you were stuck in Edinburgh by the storms."

"Oh, they were mostly further north, but it did interfere with the railways. I had to threaten my way on, invoking the name of the Duke of Kelburn."

She smiled. "No, you didn't."

"I almost did." He took back her hand and led her into the drawing room, which was quite warm, considering.

She bustled about, pushing him into the chair closest to the fire and removing the guard to add more coal. She lit the lamps and closed the curtains and announced she would make tea and reheat the dinner Cook had left for them.

But he caught her hand once more. "Not yet." He drew her into his lap, placed his hand behind her head, and searched her face. "First, a kiss." He took it, long, fervent, and unutterably sweet. "Then, perhaps," he murmured against her lips, "a glass of brandy while you tell me everything."

She closed her eyes, resting her forehead against his. "I'm so glad you are home," she whispered.

"So am I." The caress of his fingers on her nape made her shiver, and not just because they were still cold.

She slipped off his lap and went to pour two glasses of brandy. By the time she returned, he had drawn the sofa nearer the fire and sat there instead. With a sigh of bliss, she settled down beside him, his arm around her, her head on his shoulder.

They clinked glasses lazily, and each took a sip of the fine brandy that had been her father's gift to them.

Dragan touched her lips with one fingertip. "Now," he suggested.

So, she told him everything, from finding the smiling dead man at the door to imagining Dragan as his ghost. She had almost forgotten her worry that Dragan, like the inspector, would imagine she had to know the corpse, and now it seemed ridiculous, for Dragan simply listened, frowning slightly.

"It sounds to me like a very sudden death," he murmured when she had finished. "Not something that happened over the course of the night. Even if he had been there when you first went to bed, I imagine he was already dead. You could not have saved him."

How did he know that was the worst of the whole situation for her?

Because he is my Dragan. She buried her face in his neck and kissed him.

"Although," he went on, thoughtfully, drawing her closer, "that does not explain why he was sitting quite so comfortably at the door. As if he were waiting for someone he knew would come. Did Vicky bark during the night?"

"No, but then when she's at the back of the house, she doesn't much bother with what goes on at the front. She is a hopeless guard dog. Inspector Harris said he would let me know the cause of death, but the autopsy probably won't be done until after Christmas now. But I have been wondering about poison. Christmas roses are poisonous if ingested. He could have drunk some kind of infusion of it, perhaps, and with some other weakness of the stomach succumbed."

"Do you mean suicide?"

"Possibly. But why here? Everything comes back to that."

"It does." He shifted restlessly. "But your Christmas rose seems an inefficient poison, either for murder or suicide, whatever its personal significance might be. A flower of any kind is really a token of love, is it not? What if he brought a Christmas rose—or a whole bunch of them—to give to his love?"

"And a fallen petal stayed with him? And the lady who received his flower brought one for him, too, several hours later when he was already dead? She must have known he was dead when she brought the flower. If she had met him last night, she could hardly expect him to be waiting in the cold for her until the following morning. Unless the first meeting was somewhere else, and *then* he came here?"

Dragan shook his head. "No, if he had walked here, the petal would surely have fallen off. It could only have remained on his clothing because he was sitting down and didn't move."

Griz nodded. "So the assignation had to be here at our front door. Why? There is no reason unless someone, presumably Sebastian Cartaret, thought the object of his love still lived here. One of Mrs. Westley's household. A maid?"

"An unlikely object of such romantic behavior. If he loved her, he'd set her up in a discreet house somewhere, not secretly bring Christmas roses to an assignation two nights before Christmas."

"She doesn't have to be a lover," Griz objected. "What if his illegitimate daughter worked for Mrs. Westley? He is reputed to be a bon viveur."

"He is also reputed to be generous. Would such a man leave his daughter in domestic service and consider a bunch of flowers at Christmas enough acknowledgment?"

"Probably not," Griz admitted. "Though perhaps she is stubbornly independent. Perhaps he only just discovered her existence." She took another sip of brandy and glanced up at him. "Or perhaps his lover is not the maid, but Mrs. Westley."

"She could have killed him to keep her husband from finding out. Or because he was abandoning her."

"Or perhaps *Mr.* Westley found out and came in her place," Griz said, sitting up. "Snatched the flowers meant for his wife and killed him, somehow."

"And when he told his wife, she brought the flower as her last gift." Dragan examined his brandy, then drank it thoughtfully. "Other people's emotions are hard to judge. Everyone has secrets." His gaze came back to rest on her. "Perhaps we should eat."

They went to the kitchen together to reheat the casserole Cook had left for them and to feed Vicky. There, they opened a bottle of wine, and Dragan told her all about his railway journey to Edinburgh and some of the new ideas he had learned from the lectures he had attended and his discussions with the professors there.

Since there was no one to object, they ate dinner in the kitchen where it was warm and kept talking, catching up on a month apart that letters had not been able to fully account for. Then, hand in hand, they walked back toward the drawing room, and Griz, her heart beating faster, began to think of all the other things letters couldn't make up for. Surely it was bedtime?

Perhaps Dragan was thinking the same, for his thumb caressed her palm, and even in the candlelight she could see that particular glow about the eyes that made her go weak at the knees in anticipation.

A knock battered against the door, making her jump visibly.

Dragan swore beneath his breath and dropped her hand. "Wait here," he murmured and strode toward the door. Griz curled her fingers around the heavy lamp on the hall table and followed him.

Dragan opened the door, paused, then drew it wider and stood back.

Inspector Harris walked in. "Merry Christmas," he said mildly. "Glad to see you home, Tizsa."

The relationship between Dragan and the inspector was complicated—mainly by their original meeting when Dragan had been arrested for murder. Since then, a mutual, if reluctant, respect had grown, and to Dragan, Harris was a friend. To Inspector Harris, however, she suspected they were both incomprehensible—a foreign revolutionary refugee married to a duke's daughter who could not leave criminal puzzles alone.

"Merry Christmas to you," Dragan replied while Griz set down the lamp. "And I'm very glad to be home. I hope this is a social call."

"Why?" Harris demanded.

"Because I hate to think of you working so late on Christmas Eve. Your wife will miss you."

"Let me take your coat and hat," Griz offered.

"No, I can't stay. I'm on my way home," the inspector said gruffly.

"Have a quick glass of brandy with us, then." Dragan ushered him into the drawing room.

While Dragan went to pour the brandy, Harris caught Grizelda's eye and raised his brow interrogatively. For a moment, she was baffled by the silent question and then both amused and annoyed together. And very slightly touched.

"I have told Dragan all about the body at the door," she said gravely. How could he have thought otherwise? And yet, she had wanted to solve the mystery before Dragan came home because she had imagined his suspicion. It all seemed silly, now. Everything got off-kilter now when Dragan was not near. "Do you have news?"

"Thank you." Inspector Harris accepted the glass from Dragan.

They all Merry Christmas-ed again and sipped while the iInspector glanced around the room, taking in the decorations that had made their appearance since he was last here. His gaze lingered on the vase of Christmas roses.

"Our doctor performed the autopsy very quickly," Harris said bluntly. "Mr. Cartaret had an enlarged heart."

"He died of natural causes," Dragan said.

"His family was not aware of it, but the doctor thinks Cartaret himself must have been. His death will have been sudden and quick. You don't seem surprised to hear his name, my lady."

"I did peek at one of his cards while I was waiting for you," she said brazenly. "But it didn't help at the time. I know a little more about him now."

"Well, it is no longer a police matter. His remains have been returned to his family." Inspector Harris took another mouthful of brandy and set down his glass. "And I must get back to mine. Good night, Tizsas."

"Compliments of the season to your family," Dragan returned, accompanying him to the front door.

Griz sat down by the fire, mulling over the news with both relief and puzzlement. No one had killed Sebastian Cartaret. He had suffered from heart disease, and a sudden attack had carried him off. If he had made any sounds of pain, Griz had not heard them. And it would have made no difference if she had. She could not have saved him. No one could.

"But what in the world was he doing *here*?" she said aloud.

"Attending his last assignation, I suspect," Dragan replied, wandering into the room and throwing himself into the chair beside her. He reached for her hand, which she gave willingly.

"Because he knew he was going to die soon? Only I don't suppose he guessed it would be quite *that* soon, or he wouldn't have caused a potential scandal by expiring at the front door of his lady love. As he imagined," Griz added hastily.

Dragan caught her gaze. "Did you think I would suspect you?"

"Of forming such a liaison in the month you were gone? Funnily enough, it did cross my mind. Probably because it seemed to cross the inspector's. And yet, as soon as I saw you, I knew it would never enter your head."

His fingers caressed her wrist, making her shiver. "Did you? And yet you fell in love with me very quickly."

"You are *you*." She searched his face. "Then it *has* crossed your mind?"

He shook his head. "Your greeting alone told me all I wanted or needed to know. You still love me."

"And you still love me, even though I am beginning to look like a whale and have been grumpy and tearful."

He drew their joined hands to her belly and rested them there, lightly. "It is selfish of me, I know, but I like that you shed tears when I leave. I love all my time with you. And this little creature, whoever they turn out to be, is another adventure together. I will make mistakes, with you, with the child, but there will never be a lack of love."

She swallowed the sudden lump in her throat. "I never want us, either of us, to end alone outside a stranger's door in the dark, with only a flower to remind us of love."

"One of us must die first and leave the other alone. But not yet, Griz. Not yet." His sudden kiss was tender, releasing the tears to trickle beneath her spectacles and down her cheeks.

She drew back far enough to take off her glasses and wipe her face surreptitiously on his shoulder. "Do you think that is why he came here? The memory of a dead love?"

"Then who brought him the pink rose? But I can't think of them now. I can only think of you. Will you come to bed with me, Griz?"

"Yes, please."

They rose hand in hand and doused the lamps, leaving only the one candle to light their way to bed. Grizelda's heart drummed. Every nerve was aware of him as never before. A month was, by far, the longest parting they had endured since they had met, and it made him both strange and achingly familiar. Her skin tingled beneath the idle caress of his thumb on her wrist. She had never known such intense excitement before, not even on their first night together. But then, of course, she had not really understood what physical love entailed, what varied and breathless pleasures of the flesh were possible, how beautiful and inventive a man's body could be.

Now she had several months' experience of Dragan's relentless yet tender passion, and her desire grew hot and heavy, making it difficult to breathe. He left her to tend the bedchamber fire while she lit the bedside lamp and blew out her candle.

When she turned, his coat and waistcoat were already flung higgledy-piggledy on the floor, and he was tugging off his tie and collar as he advanced upon her as if he could no longer bear not to be touching her. And yet, the hands that seized her were gentle, loosening the hooks of her gown. Only his lips on hers were urgent, demanding.

"Oh, Dragan, I have missed you," she whispered into his mouth.

"Then come to bed and let me show how much I have missed

you…"

It began with slow, intimate caresses, almost like a relearning. Without words, she knew they both wanted to savor this loving. And yet, once begun, urgency took over, wild, quick, and utterly blissful.

And afterward, as they lay sated in each other's arms, she smiled and murmured against his shoulder, "God rest us merry…"

CHAPTER SIX

O F COURSE, THE morning was a different matter. Griz woke to a long, languorous loving, a tender giving and receiving of pleasure that was their long-awaited gift to each other.

It was Christmas. They were alone together in an empty house with no one to disturb them or even expect anything of them. Now that he was home, this was exactly the fun she had imagined it would be.

They rose together, eventually, rambling about the house in dressing gowns. Griz released Vicky into the garden, while Dragan stoked the stove and made coffee, and between them, they cooked breakfast to eat in bed, a naughty, childish luxury like a midnight feast she recalled with her siblings, although with Dragan, what came after was not childish at all.

When at last they washed and dressed each other, it was almost midday, and past time to begin roasting the goose Cook had prepared for them before she left. When the bird was in the oven, they danced around the kitchen for a little and then decided to take Vicky for a walk while their meal cooked.

"I have a gift for you first," Dragan said, producing a small box from his pocket.

She took it, smiling, and fished her own gift to him from behind the vase.

Grizelda's family had never been short of money, and her father kept her generous allowance going even after her marriage since Dragan's earnings were little and erratic by comparison. As a result, to save embarrassment, their gifts to each other were never ostentatious or expensive, tending more toward the amusing or the token.

For Christmas, she had bought him a small gold and sapphire tie-pin, simply because it had caught her eye. It had cost more than her other gifts, but she wanted him to have it. Still, she didn't really want him to notice its quality.

She opened the box he had given her and found a silver ring, dulled with age but exquisitely engraved with Celtic designs.

"Oh, Dragan," she breathed, drawing it from its velvet nest. "It's beautiful."

"It's very old, and I suspect worth a lot more than I paid, but I thought you would like it."

"I love it." She slid it onto her little finger, where it fitted perfectly, as she showed him, smiling.

He took her hand and kissed her fingers. "And this is the smartest pin I've ever owned. Perhaps you would oblige me?"

"I hoped it would suit you, soon-to-be Dr. Tizsa, who already has a salaried if the occasional position of great seriousness with Her Majesty's government."

"Sometimes my own importance overwhelms me." He took the opportunity of holding her while she placed the pin and patted his lapels.

"Most festive," she approved and kissed his lips.

"Thank you," he murmured and took a longer kiss, a pursuit from which they were distracted by an unexpected knock on the door.

Vicky barked and stalked out of the room as though with disapproval.

"Who could this be?" Griz wondered, slipping from his arms. "Dr. Cordell, perhaps?"

"I imagine he is busy with his own family," Dragan replied, admiring his pin in the mirror while Griz went to the door.

On the doorstep stood Elizabeth Westley.

Griz blinked in amazement. "Mrs. Westley!"

"Merry Christmas," the lady said with a somewhat tentative smile. Her voice was nervous, too. "My housekeeper just told me that your husband was away, and I did not like the idea of you being alone over Christmas. So, I spoke to my husband and my daughters, and we would all be honored if you would care to join us for Christmas luncheon."

"Oh, how kind! Please, come in."

"I called myself, to be sure you would know I mean the invitation. I—" She broke off as Dragan appeared at the drawing room door, holding Vicky.

"Dragan came home last night," Griz explained. "Please, will you join us in a glass of sherry?"

"Oh, no, I am intruding, and from the delicious smells, I gather you already have your own luncheon underway."

"True, but it is not nearly ready to eat," Dragan said, dropping Vicky to the floor so that she could delicately sniff Mrs. Westley's skirts.

"I was thinking about you, actually," Griz said, urging her into the drawing room. "After my visit to you yesterday, I wanted to tell you that the man I found apparently died of heart disease. It was likely to have been sudden in the end, although the symptoms were probably already known to him."

Mrs. Westley's eyelids drooped. She turned away to receive the glass of sherry Dragan presented to her.

She tried to smile. It was not a bad effort, but her voice was hoarse. "Merry Christmas."

When they had all sipped, she lowered her glass and raised her gaze to Dragan's. "You are a doctor, are you not? Do you think he was in pain?"

"At the end, yes, he must have been. But not for long."

She looked around as if she didn't know what to do with herself, and Griz indicated the nearest chair. They all sat.

"His name was Sebastian Cartaret," Mrs. Westley said suddenly. "I think you already knew that."

Griz nodded and waited, afraid almost to breathe in case it prevented the revelation she knew hovered on her guest's lips.

"He has so long been my secret guilt," Mrs. Westley said. "My first love, you know." She smiled nervously at Griz. "Do you still remember yours?"

Griz smiled back. "Yes." Hers was Dragan, of course, but it would hardly be kind to say so at this moment.

Mrs. Westley's smile faded. "I should not have left him there at your door. I never would if I had realized you were alone in the house. It is just my husband, you see. I could not bear him to know, to think…"

When she lapsed into silence, Griz prompted her. "How did you know Mr. Cartaret?"

"I met him first when I was just seventeen years old, and he, all of five and twenty. It was my first Season, and he made everything special. He was handsome and kind and full of laughter and fun. Everyone said he was wild, but there was no malice in him. He was merely one of these people who are full of joy in life. He was…dazzling."

A smile of memory flickered across her lips. "And I was dazzled. He proposed marriage to me, and I accepted, but we had reckoned without our families. His was an old name, but like many landed families, including my own, they had fallen on bad times. And he was a younger son. I was told he had no prospects, that he could not keep a wife, let alone keep a wife well. They told me he was a rake who would never be faithful and make my life miserable with humiliation and poverty. Instead, my father wanted me to accept a different offer.

From Mr. Westley."

"I see," Griz murmured.

The older woman's eyes refocused on her face briefly. "I'm not sure you do. You seem to have the courage of your convictions." Her gaze flickered to Dragan and back. "I did not. Sebastian said we should ignore them all and marry anyway. His own father told him he was lazy and would never amount to anything good in the world. My father said William had better prospects and more character. And even though I knew Sebastian had taken a position in a bank and promised to work hard and be true... I was not. I allowed myself to be worn down, to be persuaded that William Westley was the better match."

"Was he?" Griz asked.

"How can I compare it? To this day, I hardly know Sebastian. He is a dream of the past, an illusion. William was my reality." She stirred uncomfortably in her chair. "I do not want you to think my life with him was difficult, for it was not. He is a good man, a lovable man, and I did grow to love him and our life together, quite sincerely. We have two beautiful daughters." She caught Grizelda's eye again. "You are newly wed and cannot know, but trust me when I say there is nothing, *nothing* that brings you closer than the shared joy in one's children."

Instinctively, Griz laid her hand across her belly, feeling suddenly protective and *loving*. The gesture was lost on Mrs. Westley, who had clearly returned to the world of her own memory. But Dragan saw.

"And Sebastian?" Griz prompted.

"Oh, Sebastian confounded all his critics. I have no idea how hard he worked at it, but he must have had aptitude, for he quickly soared up the ranks of the bank staff until he became a partner himself, began to invest in all sorts of other successful ventures. He could easily, if he chose, buy up my father and his own, and William, too."

"Did you ever wonder," Dragan asked as she lapsed into silence once more, "if you had made a mistake?"

"Oh, no," Mrs. Westley replied. "I was glad for Sebastian when I learned of his success, but my life was with William and the girls."

"And yet you talk of guilt," Griz pointed out.

Mrs. Westley sighed and finished her sherry in one surprising gulp. Wordlessly, Dragan rose, fetched the decanter, and refilled her glass. She didn't appear to notice.

"In the first year of my marriage, on the anniversary of the day he proposed to me—Christmas Eve—I found a single Christmas rose outside the front door of my marital home. This house. It had been built by William's father for his widowed grandmother, and when she died, it became vacant and was a sensible place for us to live."

Presumably rent-free, Griz thought cynically.

"I never told William, even when the second rose appeared the following year. By chance, I had caught the first one before anyone else saw it, and after that, I watched for them, brought them in, and placed them in a vase somewhere around the house. No one ever commented, and I never told William. I was afraid he would be jealous or think it improper, even confront Sebastian about it. I didn't want that. I wanted the excitement, the proof of Sebastian's continued devotion, even though I was happy in my marriage."

"*That* is your guilt?" Griz said slowly. "A little selfish, harmless romance?"

"It was to me. I had no idea what it meant to Sebastian, for I never spoke to him, never even saw him from the day we parted. But William and I had never discussed him. I was never entirely sure he would understand. I'm still not. In any case, with the passage of the years, I learned that he brought the rose round about midnight, so I collected it before I went to bed, and no one was ever any the wiser. It was a simple matter while we lived here."

"And then you moved into the bigger house," Dragan guessed.

"Exactly. It was not so simple to time, and I misjudged." She drew in an unsteady breath. "I took a lantern, crept out of my own home, and hurried up the path to yours. And there he sat in the moonlight, a single, white Christmas rose in his hand.

"It was twenty years since I had seen him, even in the dark, and I confess my heartbeat quickened. I don't know what I meant to do, but he had seen the light from my lantern and said my name. *Lizzie.*"

She smiled softly, sadly. "No one else ever called me Lizzie. I couldn't help it. I went to him, and I saw that he was in pain. But even so, he smiled at me, just as he had when we were young and foolish and so in love…"

A single tear escaped the corner of her eye and trickled down her cheek. She didn't seem to notice. "He died with that smile on his face," she whispered, "for me."

With a hint of desperation, she raised her glass and drank. So did Griz.

Dragan said, "So you took the rose he had brought for you."

"I have them all still, pressed between the pages of novels and other books I know William will never read. I no longer loved Sebastian—how could I? But I loved his fidelity over those twenty years. It made *me* feel good."

"I'm sure that's what he intended," Dragan said. "But without the guilt."

She looked at him. "I did think that once he was dead, the guilt would vanish. There can be no more Christmas roses, no more to hide from my husband." With a gasp, she finished her sherry and stood. "I did not mean to tell you all this. I have never told anyone and hope you will keep my confidence."

"Of course." Dragan, being a gentleman, had risen also. "But I think you did mean to tell my wife at least. To assuage that guilt."

"It has not worked." Mrs. Westley set down her glass.

"Because you are telling the wrong people," Griz said gently. "It is your husband you want to tell."

Mrs. Westley swung to face her, looking stricken. "I cannot do that to William! To me!"

"Some secrets can help one stay sane or independent," Griz remarked. "Others can seep poison into something that is good and dear."

Mrs. Westley stared at her for a long moment, and she was afraid she had gone too far. "You look too young," she said slowly, "to have such wisdom."

"I'm not wise," Griz protested. "Just observant. And interfering. You know your own husband best and must decide for yourself."

"As a mature woman, soon to be a grandmother, rather than as a young, spoiled debutante?" Mrs. Westley smiled quickly, "No, don't answer that. Perhaps it is time I reconsidered. It is definitely time I left. But you are both welcome to join us, if not for luncheon, then later in the day, perhaps."

"Perhaps we will," Dragan said. "Thank you for the invitation."

CHAPTER SEVEN

"WELL," DRAGAN SAID as Griz returned to his side after their guest's departure. "Your mystery appears to be solved. To your satisfaction?"

"I don't know whether to be happy or unbearably sad."

"I vote for happy. I gather Mr. Cartaret always was."

"Outwardly, at least. Imagine him carrying a torch for Mrs. Westley all those years."

"It probably got a little like a habit after the first year or so," Dragan remarked. "A harking back to the innocent romance of his youth."

"Was he really smiling at her, or was it some kind of death grimace? No, don't tell me. I'd rather think of it as a smile. I believe he was happy to see her before he died."

"And that is what Mrs. Westley believes, too."

Griz nodded.

Dragan's hand covered hers in her lap. "You gave her good advice. About secrets."

She gazed at their joined hands, saying nothing.

"Griz," he said softly. "I know you are afraid to have this baby. You don't need to hide it from me. I have been learning all I can about childbirth and post-natal fevers, so—"

"No, no, you have it wrong, Dragan," she burst out, twisting her hand under his to grasp his fingers. "My fears are not of physical harm. I quite rely on you to keep me and the baby alive through whatever

God or nature throws at us."

A frown tugged at his brow as he searched her face. "You were not ready. You did not want to have a child so soon."

Her grip tightened. "I was afraid it would come between us," she admitted. "I love my life with you, all our adventures, mysteries, and puzzles. I don't want to stop doing those things, being all those things to you. And the baby will need me."

"I love our life, too. I'm sorry it is coming too soon for you. I should have taken more care, made fewer demands."

"I love your demands!" She freed her hand but only to throw both arms around his neck. "I was afraid of change. *Was*. But somehow—I think I realized this only when Mrs. Westley was speaking—somehow, I have come to love the little creature inside me, and I realized this does not *stop* the adventure but adds to it. For both of us. I have been confused, alternately fearful, and joyful and fearful again. I should have known I could not keep that from you, and I wish I had not tried."

His arms came around her. And in that moment, perhaps feeling the pressure against her abdomen, the baby moved.

Griz gasped and drew back, dragging his hand to where she had felt the funny little kick. They gazed at each other in wonder.

"God rest you merry, little Tizsa," Dragan said softly.

And Grizelda's world had never seemed so happy or so complete.

LATE THAT NIGHT, well-fed on goose and spicy Christmas pudding, Griz and Dragan took Vicky for a last walk. Heading for the Green Park on the other side of Piccadilly, they inevitably passed the Westleys' House.

Griz could not help looking upward, and there in the brightly lit window, she saw Mrs. Westley, her face stained with tears.

"Oh no," Griz whispered. Saddened, she would have hurried on, but Dragan held her still a moment longer. Which is how she saw the figure of Mr. Westley appear and put his arms around his wife. She collapsed against him, clutching him to her, and Griz smiled, though a lump formed in her throat. "She has told him. And all is well."

"I think so," Dragan agreed, drawing her onward.

Griz walked beside him in the cold beauty of winter, for once not marred by freezing fog. She felt warm and contented and excited about the future. Her eyes might have misted a little as she sent up a silent prayer for Sebastian Cartaret. But hugging Dragan's arm, she could not grieve long for a stranger on such a night. They were blessed.

She smiled into the night. *God rest us merry, indeed.*

About Mary Lancaster

Mary Lancaster lives in Scotland with her husband, three mostly grown-up kids and a small, crazy dog.

Her first literary love was historical fiction, a genre which she relishes mixing up with romance and adventure in her own writing. Her most recent books are light, fun Regency romances written for Dragonblade Publishing: *The Imperial Season* series set at the Congress of Vienna; and the popular *Blackhaven Brides* series, which is set in a fashionable English spa town frequented by the great and the bad of Regency society.

Connect with Mary on-line – she loves to hear from readers:

Email Mary:
Mary@MaryLancaster.com

Website:
www.MaryLancaster.com

Newsletter sign-up:
http://eepurl.com/b4Xoif

Facebook:
facebook.com/mary.lancaster.1656

Facebook Author Page:
facebook.com/MaryLancasterNovelist

Twitter:
@MaryLancNovels

Amazon Author Page:
amazon.com/Mary-Lancaster/e/B00DJ5IACI

Bookbub:
bookbub.com/profile/mary-lancaster

Printed in Great Britain
by Amazon

57528535R00036